DRAGON and THE RABBITS

Gina Fales.

BY LUCY KINCAID

ILLUSTRATED BY ERIC KINCAID

and Kristle

BRIMAX BOOKS · NEWMARKET · ENGLAND

Dragon lives in the wood. He hums songs with the bees.
The baby rabbits want to hum too. They do not know how to hum.

Dragon stops humming.
"Go away, and play," says
Dragon.
The bees stop humming.
"Go away, and play," say
the bees.
The baby rabbits hop
away.
They hop into the wood.

Dragon is humming again.
The bees are humming again.
Along comes Mother Rabbit.
"Where are my babies?" says Mother Rabbit.
"I do not know," says Dragon.
"We do not know," say the bees.

Mother Rabbit calls her babies. They do not come. Mother Rabbit begins to cry.

"I have lost my babies," she says.

"Do not cry," says Dragon. "We will find your babies for you," say the bees.

They all look for the baby
rabbits.
Dragon looks for them.
The bees look for them.
Mother Rabbit looks for
them.
The baby rabbits have
gone.
Nobody can see them.
"They must be hiding,"
says Dragon.

Dragon stops. He stands still.
"Listen," says Dragon. "I can hear something."
"So can I," says Mother Rabbit.
"So can we," say the bees.

Dragon peeps over the
bush.
He can see something.
"Come here," says Dragon.
The bees look over the
bush.
Mother Rabbit looks over
the bush.

The baby rabbits are
sitting on the grass.
"What are they doing?"
say the bees.
The baby rabbits are trying
to hum.
They are trying very hard.
But they cannot do it.

"Hallo!" says Dragon.
"What are you trying to do?"
The baby rabbits see Dragon.
They hop away and hide.
"Come out of there," says Dragon.

The baby rabbits will not come out of the hole. They do not see Mother Rabbit. "Come out of there at once," says Mother Rabbit. "Yes, Mother," say the baby rabbits.

"Come with me," says Mother Rabbit. "We are going home."
The baby rabbits look very sad.
"What were they trying to do?" say the bees.
"They were trying to hum, like us," says Dragon.

"We can show them how
to hum," say the bees.
"Yes," says Dragon.
It takes a long time to
show a rabbit how to hum.
Dragon tries very hard.
So do the bees.
At last they do it.

Dragon is humming.
The bees are humming.
The rabbits are humming.
"I did not know rabbits
could hum," says Owl.
"My babies are the only
rabbits who can," says
Mother Rabbit.

Say these words again

Mother	know
baby	bush
babies	listen
rabbit	trying
once	where
something	show
could	hear